Tucker Goes to Heaven

A Children's Book

Written by Alicia Bausley
Illustrated by Hayako Otsubo

Llumina Kids

Requests for permission to make copies of any part of this work should be mailed to Permissions Department, Llumina Kids, PO Box 772246, Coral Springs, FL 33077-2246

ISBN: 1-59526-457-4

Printed in the United States of America by Llumina Kids

Library of Congress Control Number: 2006906413

Tucker Goes to Heaven

Dedication

This book is dedicated to sweet Tucker, an English springer spaniel, who was a wonderful gift from Jesus, our Father, and the Holy Spirit. May all the children and doggies in heaven get the chance to know Tucker's wonderful gift of love and loyalty. For all who have loved and lost a pet, I hope this book brings peace and comfort to your heart.

And, to my husband, Ben, who has taught me the true meaning of love, guided me in my spiritual journey, and encouraged me to dream and reach for the stars of heaven.

Alicia Bausley

Tucker was a beautiful English springer spaniel dog. His fur coat was shiny milk chocolate brown and snow white, and dark chocolate spots speckled his white coat. He had the prettiest long silky brown ears, which fanned out across the floor while he slept. Tucker's eyelashes were very thick and long, and when he closed his eyes, his lashes would flutter on his snoot! At ten-years-old, he was quite elderly in doggy years, still able to run and play, but at a much slower pace than when he was a puppy. Tucker was very well behaved and always did all that his mommy and daddy told him to do. This was important, so that one day his goodness would take him to heaven!

Alicia Bausley

S wimming was Tucker's most favorite thing to do in the whole world. Everyday he stuck his big furry front paw into the water of the swimming pool to see if the water was cold. He knew he could not go in for a swim unless his parents were nearby to watch over him. So he would wait and wait until his mommy would come out to sit by the pool and give her nod of approval. But before he would dive into the swimming pool, Tucker would do one more paw-test.

Once more, just to make sure the water was perfect, Tucker stuck his great white paw into the swimming pool to find that the water was just right! He looked over at his mommy and she smiled and told him, "Yes, Tucker, you can go in." As soon as she gave him the okay, Tucker took a running start, and with all four paws flying in the air, he jumped into the swimming pool and made a wonderful wet splash. The water was cold, just how he liked it! He loved swimming and especially liked the first jump into the swimming pool. As the water tickled his nose and whiskers, Tucker paddled towards his favorite toy.

His sleek wet head came out of the water and his big brown eyes searched eagerly for his red ball. When he saw the ball floating lazily across the pool, Tucker swam and swam as hard as he could to reach it. All four of his paws kicked furiously beneath him. When he reached his ball, he grabbed it with his mouth and cheerfully brought it out of the water to his mommy, with his short stubby tail wagging furiously behind him. Then, as all doggies do to dry off, Tucker turned his head back and forth and worked into a big hearty shake of his delightfully wet body, swishing this way and that way so that water splashed everywhere. Even on his mommy!

On other days, Tucker rode in the car. He loved to ride in the front seat with the window down. Tucker always stuck his head out the window and let the breeze blow through his whiskers. He delighted in the whistling sound of the wind hitting his ears! His eyes squinted, his ears flapped in the breeze, and his mouth dripped with doggy drool. Even though his nose would tickle, he loved every single minute of his car ride.

Another fun game was playing Frisbee with Daddy. Tucker watched intently as the Frisbee sailed through the air, and then he ran as hard as his doggy legs could to catch the Frisbee in mid air. Tucker pranced and marched the Frisbee back to his daddy, as proud as could be, because he had done such a good job! Then, after a hard game of Frisbee, Tucker enjoyed a favorite mouth-watering snack.

Tucker loved to eat. He was very patient as he waited by the refrigerator, looking intently at the door, almost as though he could see right through it! Just in time to hear his stomach growl and gurgle, his mommy entered the room and told him it was time for dinner. Hurray! Tucker gobbled up his dinner and then waited patiently for the treat his mommy always gave to him after dinner. Mommy made the best doggy French fries. Oh, how delicious those French fries tasted. He offered his paw to mommy to thank her. Now it was time to think of new doggy tricks.

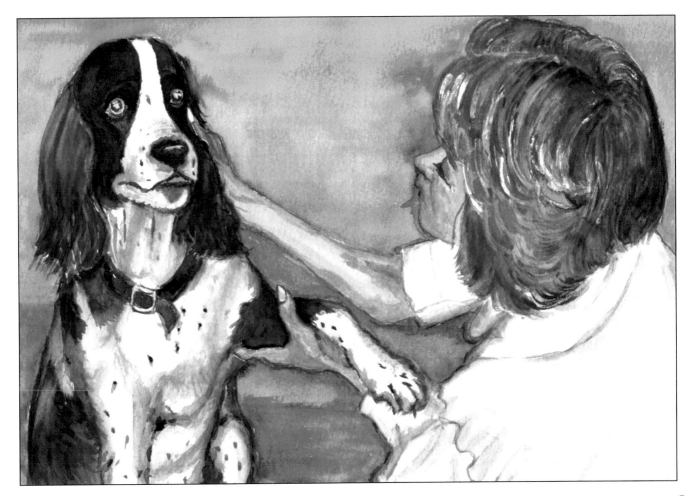

A very special day for Tucker was to teach Daddy new doggy tricks. Tucker loved to sit when he was told and to shake with his paw when his Daddy asked him to shake hands. His most favorite trick was giving Dad the high-five by throwing his left paw in the air and smacking it into Dad's hand. This always made Daddy laugh It even made Tucker laugh! Tucker had the biggest doggy smile, showing off his little pearly white front teeth. Playing high-five made Tucker laugh almost as much as chasing light beams.

Tucker wore a soft red leather collar with a silver buckle. When he went outside to play, the light reflected off the buckle and shined down onto the ground. Tucker loved to chase that light all over the place. It was amazing how quickly that light moved! It seemed that every time Tucker moved, the light moved! Tucker did not know that the beautiful shining light would return to him on another day to take him to a very special place.

One sunny afternoon, Tucker did not feel very well. He was very achy and tired. He did not want to swim, and he did not want to eat. Days turned into weeks and he did not feel any better, in fact, he did not feel well at all. He laid his tired body in his soft warm bed and had no energy to play with his toys.

On one of those days while he was busy sleeping and dreaming, a beautiful glorious white light appeared. It was an intriguing light, which mesmerized Tucker until he began to chase the light in his dream. Around and around he chased the pretty light, his ears swung side to side and back and forth. However, unlike the other times when the light escaped him while he played, this time he caught the light, and when he did, it turned into a magnificent angel from heaven.

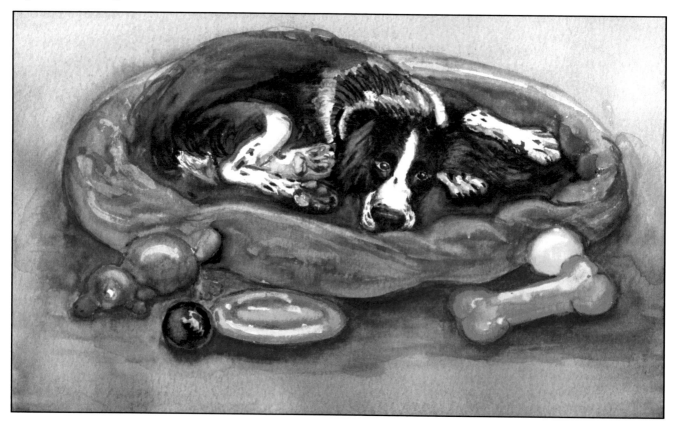

The splendid angel had pretty graceful wings, a silky white and blue flowing robe, and a soft, kind, and tender face. She touched Tucker's head to wake him and told him he was going to heaven. "But I don't want to go to heaven," Tucker said. I want to feel better and swim in my pool, play with my ball, and go for a car ride! But the angel insisted that Jesus wanted Tucker to come to heaven. Jesus needed Tucker in heaven to do something very special.

Tucker thought he was too tired to go to heaven, because he did not feel well. The angel promised him that he would soon feel wonderful. "Have faith, little Tucker," the angel told him. "Jesus will provide you with strength, energy, and lots of love." Tucker cried, "But, I will miss my mommy and daddy." The angel assured Tucker that his mommy and daddy would understand, and that one day, they too would be with Tucker in heaven. "Look into my face and trust me," the angel said.

Tucker slowly got up from his bed, and amazingly he felt wonderful! He could not believe it! He stretched his paw out long and hard and then he stretched his other paw out. He yawned and turned his head this way and that way and finally he gave a GREAT BIG shake of his body.

"Oh boy! I feel like a *puppy dog* again!" shouted Tucker. The angel lovingly smiled at Tucker and took his paw in her hand and slowly they started their climb to heaven. Tucker was so excited. For the first time in months, he felt really good and he did not feel tired or achy. He could not wait to see Jesus in heaven.

The angel held tightly onto Tucker as they drifted up into the white clouds above the blue sky, over the trees, over the mountains, and to the gates of heaven. When they reached heaven's gate, the angel let go of Tucker's paw. Then Tucker heard someone call his name. Because he finally felt and looked like his young puppy self again, he ran quickly across the cloud, and excitedly pushed open the beautiful gold gate to heaven. And who do you think was waiting just for him? Jesus!

Jesus was surrounded in a stunning brilliant light that splashed across the clouds. He was dressed in a dazzling white robe with brown sandals on His feet. His face showed love, compassion, and kindness and Jesus laughed with pleasure when He saw Tucker. Jesus told him, *"Tucker, my Father and I and all the angels in heaven have been waiting for you. We cannot wait to show you around heaven and introduce you to all your new friends. You will be very happy here. You will feel, act, and even look like a puppy again! You will be full of never-ending energy, run without being tired, swim, and play ball as long as you want! You will never be sick again."*

Tucker was so thrilled to hear the message from Jesus. Then Jesus gave him another surprise. Jesus stretched out His hand, took Tucker by the paw and kissed Tucker's forehead. He said, *"Tucker, I love you and I need you to do a very important task for me. It will require you to give with all your heart and doggy soul. I need you to love a little boy named Daniel who just arrived in heaven last night."*

Tucker was thrilled and honored to do a special job for Jesus. Tucker, while bathing in the beautiful light from Jesus, panted, jumped, and pawed at the ground. He gave a great big Tucker smile to Jesus, showing his little white teeth, and shouted to Him, "I can do it! I can do it!"

Jesus smiled back at Tucker and explained to him, *"On earth Daniel had been a very sick little boy. He was eight years old when he left his mommy and daddy to come to heaven and now he needs a special friend. He needs you Tucker, to be his friend, to love him, play ball with him, and go swimming with him."* Tucker wagged his tail, shaking his whole body with happiness. He followed closely at the feet of Jesus to meet his new friend, Daniel.

Daniel was a special little boy who had been loved very much by his mommy and daddy. His hair was blonde and his eyes were bright blue. He had a smile that lit up all of heaven. As soon as Daniel saw Tucker, he laughed in pure pleasure and joy. He reached out his hands, got down on his knees, and called for Tucker to come to him. Tucker, happy to oblige, ran to Daniel. He licked Daniel's face and he let Daniel wrap his arms around his brown and white speckled neck and kiss his soft-whiskered puppy snoot.

Daniel turned to Jesus and asked if it would be alright to go swimming in heaven's pool. Jesus told Daniel, "You may swim *for as long as you want. Take Tucker and enjoy your new friend. I promise that you will be happy here in heaven and always be loved and cherished. You and Tucker were good on earth and now you may enjoy My Father's reward of heaven."*

How exciting! Tucker and Daniel ran side-by-side to heaven's pool. Tucker with his four paws ran across the green grass and Daniel with his short little legs tried to keep up. Tucker turned and waited and when Daniel was almost to him, Tucker ran and jumped into the air. Then he took off, pranced, and danced as if he were a puppy once again, and through God's miraculous powers – he was!

magine their surprise when they got to heaven's pool and jumped in and hundreds of red and white balls rolled across the water. Tucker jumped, he swam, and he grabbed one red and white ball after another, each time taking them to Daniel. Daniel no longer felt the pain from being very sick and he did not feel a bit tired. They swam and then they rested on heaven's cool green grass. Daniel giggled in pure contentment and put his arms around Tucker's neck. He looked into Tucker's big brown eyes, and told him, "I love you, Tucker. Thank you for being my special friend." Tucker turned and looked into Daniel's beautiful big blue eyes; he nuzzled his snoot into Daniel's neck, and whispered in a doggy bark, "I love you, too."

Tucker, although he too missed his mommy and daddy, knew in his doggy heart that everything would be okay. He trusted Jesus and His Father and he had Daniel to care for in heaven. He knew that one day he would see his mommy and daddy again, and so would Daniel. Jesus, His Father, and all the angels in heaven would love and take care of both of their parents, until they met up in heaven with them. But for now, he had important God-work to do. Jesus had entrusted Daniel to him. This English springer spaniel was going to do his best to make Daniel the happiest little boy in heaven.

The End

Author Biography

Alicia Bausley has a life-long love and compassion for all animals on God's earth. Her soft spot for rescues frequently results in tracking down strays to help them find their way home. She vacations in Carmel by the Sea, a lovely and pet-friendly town, where her two dogs are always by her side. Majoring in communications, she graduated from California State University Fullerton. She resides in Anaheim Hills, California with her husband Ben, her English springer spaniel, Lacy, and American Staffordshire terrier, Delilah.

Illustrator's Biography

Hayako Otsubo has been a passionate follower of Jesus Christ. Her love for our Lord is exemplified in her love for not only people, but all animals, especially dogs, which is her favorite subject to paint and draw. She enjoys oil painting as a hobby and has been studying watercolor artistry. Hayako lives in Newport Beach, California, with her husband Lawrence and her golden retrievers, Joy and Josh.